this
·little·orchard·
book belongs to

....

....

ORCHARD BOOKS
96 Leonard Street, London EC2A 4RH
Orchard Books Australia
14 Mars Road, Lane Cove, NSW 2066
1 86039 536 8 (hardback)
1 86039 489 2 (paperback)
First published in Great Britain in 1997
Copyright © Nicola Smee 1997
The right of Nicola Smee to be identified as the author and illustrator of this work has been
asserted by her in accordance with the Copyright, Designs and Patents Act, 1988.
A CIP catalogue record for this book is available from the British Library.
Printed in Italy

Freddie gets dressed

Nicola Smee

• little • orchard •

My bear's bare
and so am I.
I think we'd better
get dressed.

Pants for me
and
pants for Bear.

T-shirt for me
and
T-shirt for Bear.

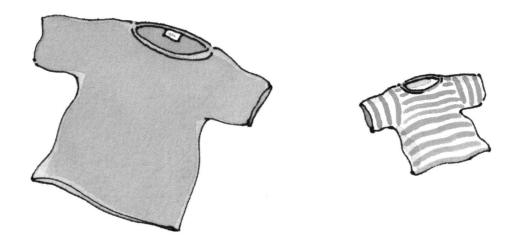

Socks for me
and
socks for Bear.

Trousers for
me and ...
I think a skirt for
Bear today.

Shoes for me
and
shoes for Bear.

Oh, no!
It's back to being bare, Bear!